I Can Read!™

My First READING

Chicken Said, "Cluck!"

by Judyann Ackerman Grant
pictures by Sue Truesdell

SCHOLASTIC INC.
New York Toronto London Auckland
Sydney Mexico City New Delhi Hong Kong

ISBN 978-0-545-23978-3

Text copyright © 2008 by Judyann Ackerman Grant.
Illustrations copyright © 2008 by Sue Truesdell.
I Can Read Book® is a trademark of HarperCollins Publishers Inc. All rights reserved.
Published by Scholastic Inc., 557 Broadway, New York, NY 10012, by arrangement with HarperCollins Children's Books, a division of HarperCollins Publishers. SCHOLASTIC and associated logos are trademarks and/or registered trademarks of Scholastic Inc.

12 11 10 9 8 7 6 5 4 3 2 1   10 11 12 13 14 15/0

Printed in the U.S.A.   40

First Scholastic printing, September 2010

To R.V.A., my Mom,
who instilled in me a love of reading
—J.A.G.

For Anne
—S.T.

"I will grow a pumpkin,"
said Earl.

"I will grow two pumpkins,"
said Pearl.

Chicken scratched the dirt.

6

"Shoo!" said Earl.

"Shoo! Shoo!" said Pearl.

"Cluck! Cluck! Cluck!"
said Chicken.

Earl dug the garden.

Pearl planted the seeds.

Chicken scratched the dirt.
"Shoo!" said Earl.

"Shoo! Shoo!" said Pearl.
"Cluck! Cluck! Cluck!"
said Chicken.

Earl watered the seeds.

Pearl pulled the weeds.

Chicken scratched the dirt.

"Shoo!" said Earl.

"Shoo! Shoo!" said Pearl.
"Cluck! Cluck! Cluck!"
said Chicken.

Earl's pumpkin grew.

Pearl's pumpkins grew.

Chicken scratched the dirt.

"Shoo!" said Earl.

"Shoo! Shoo!" said Pearl.

16

"Cluck! Cluck! Cluck!"
said Chicken.

Then one day
grasshoppers came.

Jump! In the garden.
Nibble.
Jump! On the pumpkins.
Nibble. Nibble.

Jump! Jump! Jump!
Nibble. Nibble. Nibble.

"Shoo!" said Earl.

"Shoo! Shoo!" said Pearl.

The grasshoppers stayed.

Chicken said, "Cluck!"
One grasshopper jumped.

Chicken said,

"Cluck! Cluck!"

Two grasshoppers jumped.

24

Chicken said,
"Cluck! Cluck! Cluck!"
Jump! Jump! Jump!

27

"Hooray!" said Earl.

"Hooray! Hooray!" said Pearl.

"Cluck! Cluck! Cluck!"
said Chicken.

Earl gave Chicken
one pumpkin.

Pearl gave Chicken
two pumpkins.

Chicken scratched the dirt.